Lockdown Lyrics

By

Julie Sheldon

Copyright: © 2020 Julie Sheldon
All rights reserved
ISBN: 9798690721336

Contents

4	What If It's Just Nature?	38	Don't Worry
5	Don't Be A Tosser….BIN IT!	40	Important Jobs
6	Some Of Us	42	Mirror Mirror
8	Bubble Trouble	44	The Fireplace
9	Lockdown Locks	47	Pants
11	The Same Boat	50	Just Words
13	Lost In Lockdown	51	Special Neighbour
14	Naked Attraction	53	The Cycle
16	Pamper Session	55	Housework
19	Tinned Tomatoes	57	Why?
21	It's Okay	58	Entitlement
23	Online Shopping	60	Facebook Friends
24	School Reunion	61	A Stitch In Time
26	Harley Holiday	62	What Tomorrow Brings
29	A Verse	63	Something Fishy
30	Dear Cyclist	65	Instinct
31	On Yer Bike	66	Apple Pie
32	Walking	67	Heartache
34	Positive	68	September Evening
36	Gone Fishing	69	Thankful

****

Introduction

This is a collection of poems, some humorous and some more serious, which I wrote during the first six months of the Covid19 pandemic.

In early April 2020, I was chatting to my neighbour Ann, about the corona virus, and how it might have all started.
She made a comment….."I think it's Nature"…….

That set me thinking…. "What if it's just Nature?"

There began my 'Lockdown Lyrics'

Prior to this I had only 'dabbled' in poetry, writing a few limericks and an odd verse here and there, during my younger years.

I'd like to say a huge "Thank you" to all my family, friends and even some 'strangers' who have encouraged me to put this book together……you all know who you are. I would never have done it without your support.

I have presented the poems in the order in which they were written, as I feel that this reflects my ever-changing thoughts, moods, and feelings during this unprecedented and thought-provoking time.

I hope you enjoy them!

****

*This is the first poem that I wrote during lockdown.
There began my' Lockdown Lyrics'*

What If It's Just Nature?

What if it's just Nature?
Taking back control
Questioning the actions
Of every living soul

What if it's just Nature?
Asking us to stop
To think about our planet
And treasure what we've got

What if it's just Nature?
Slowing us right down
Time to look around us
And see what can be found

What if it's just Nature?
Asking us to think
What is it that we really need?
Love, health and food and drink

What if it's just Nature?
Giving us the time
To be more understanding,
Generous and kind

What if it's just Nature?
Asking us to care
To think about each other
And sometimes just be there

What if it's just Nature?
Sending us this pain
Time to re-evaluate
Before we're all insane

What if it's just Nature?
Setting us a test
To try to save our planet
Let's do our very best!
****

During early lockdown, a young couple from the local village, started a Facebook group called ' Lockdown Litterpick Challenge', encouraging people to do a litter pick when they went on their daily walks.
The added inspiration for this poem was from a slogan that they apparently use on posters in Sydney, Australia

Don't Be A Tosser......BIN IT!

You've had your bag of toffees
And eaten all that's in it
You've drunk your cup of coffee
Don't be a tosser....BIN IT!

You've smoked your final ciggie
Your packet's got none in it
Scoffed crisps just like Miss Piggy
Don't be a tosser..... BIN IT!

You've necked your can of lager
It seems there is no limit
You've polished off a pack of four
Don't be a tosser....BIN IT!

You've bought a Lotto scratch card
You know you'll never win it
Don't throw that ticket on the floor
Don't be a tosser....BIN IT!

You've picked up after 'Poochykins'
It's really easy innit?
But then your brain goes out of gear
Don't be a tosser.....BIN IT!

Just think about the stuff you throw
Just ponder for a minute
It's really not that difficult!
Don't be a tosser......BIN IT!

****

I'm sure that all our lives were affected in some way by the 'lockdown' during the pandemic. I started to think what this may have meant for 'some of us'

Some Of Us

Some of us must stay at home
And not go out the door
Some of us are working
Like we've never worked before

Some of us are falling out
With siblings, Dads, and Mothers
Some of us are reaching out
And looking after others

Some of us are keeping busy
Doing lots of jobs
Some of us have given up......
We're turning into slobs

Some of us are playing games
And learning brand new hobbies
Some of us are still 'no good'
And watching out for 'Bobbies'

Some of us have lots of friends
To text with and to phone
Some of us have no one
And feel that we're alone

Some of us feel positive
And think that we're in charge
Some of us feel anxious
And fear the world at large

Some of us have footpaths
To cycle, walk, and jog
Some of us have nowhere nice
To even walk the dog

Some of us are welcoming
New babies being born
Some of us have lost loved ones
And cannot truly mourn

None of us will ever know
What's really going on
None of us will think the same
When all of this is done

Some of us can choose to spend
Our days in fear and dread.....but
All of us can choose to plan
For better days ahead!

****

When the government introduced 'social' or 'support' bubbles, I imagine that it was a difficult time for some, deciding who would be in their 'bubble'

Bubble Trouble

I am a single granny
With daughter, and a son
I've got a newish lover
And he's a lot of fun!

Now I can make a 'bubble'
But which house do I choose?
Someone will be offended
No matter what I do

Do I go to my daughter's?
And help wipe snotty noses
Or do I see my lover?
For candlelight and roses

Do I go to my son's house?
And risk an ear bashing
Or shall I go to lover boy's?
And have some nights of passion

And then, there's my friend Maureen
Who has nobody else
So shall I spend some time with her?
And not think of myself

Am I a granny dutiful?
On whom they can depend
Am I a selfish lover?
Or a dedicated friend?

This really is a problem
That I could do without
In fact, it was much simpler
When I could NOT go out

Oh Boris! Why've you caused me
Such a lot of trouble?
I really don't know what to do
With this flippin' 'social bubble'
****

During 'lockdown', many people unintentionally ended up with very different looking hair. Unless you lived with a hairdresser or trusted someone in your household with a pair of scissors (which unfortunately I didn't), then 'au naturelle' became the order of the day

Lockdown Locks

I've battled with my wavy hair
Since I was in my teens
It's neither straight nor curly
But somewhere in between

The good old days of 'Purdy' cuts
Caused me so much distress
I'd try to pull it into shape
But still it looked a mess

But then when perms became the 'norm'
I joined in with the fashion
But then I ended up with hair
Like 'younger' Michael Jackson

In recent times it's been quite short
The colouring's got lighter
But three months into 'lockdown'
It's looking even whiter

I used to be a dark brunette
But then it started fading
So I succumbed to colour charts
And lots of clever shading

My waves are back to haunt me
In fact it's going curly
At least the grey is blending in
....I look like Temple (Shirley)

I know that I am not alone....
One friend looks like a monk....
Another can't quite yet decide....
On badger?....or a skunk?

The thing is....now it's grown a bit
I feel a bit more girly
Should it all be cut off again?
Or do I go for curly?

And do I grow grey gracefully?
Or have it all re-dyed?
Perhaps I'll buy a wig or two
Until I can decide

****

I was listening to the radio during 'lockdown'. I heard someone say that 'we're all in the same boat'....that set me thinking.....maybe we were on the same rough sea but in lots of different boats....

The Same Boat

'We're all in the same boat' they say
But I would disagree
So many different sailing crafts
Upon this stormy sea

Some sail on ocean liners
In comfort, style, and ease
Relaxing on their balconies
Sipping their G & Ts

Some speed along in motor boats
As if it's all ok
With little care for smaller crafts
Which may get in their way

Some struggle on their battleships
Where nothing's going right
Endlessly preparing
For the next relentless fight

Some huddle in their lifeboats
And pray that they'll be saved
Hoping for a calmer sea
And fearing every wave

Some drift around upon their rafts
They barely stay afloat
They're praying for a change of luck
And chance to board a boat

Some haven't found their sea legs yet
And dread each wave and swell
They're struggling to stay upright
And don't feel very well

So whilst you're on your passage
To a safe and calmer port
Look out for fellow sailors
Who may need some support

Could you throw them a life belt?
Or a paddle, or an oar?
Perhaps you could help guide them
A bit nearer to the shore

****

It was three months into 'lockdown' and I couldn't sleep one night. I had words going through my mind so I wrote this poem at 3.30am. I think it is fair to say that during 'lockdown' a lot of people were feeling uncertain, worried, apprehensive, anxious, vulnerable......

Lost in Lockdown

We feel that we're in mourning
'Normality' seems dead
We're walking unfamiliar paths
Unsure of where to tread

We've lost our AA Road Maps
The Sat Nav's broken down
We're driving through the back streets
In the 'dodgy' part of town

We've been thrown in deep water
But we can swim no more
And now we're floating slowly
But cannot reach the shore

We're on a roller coaster
We're up and then we're down
We just want to get off now
And stand on solid ground

We need to find direction
We need to find some strength
We fear the road to 'New Normal'
Is of an unknown length

We must take some control now
We need rid of this grief
Our 'Normal' has been stolen
And Corona is the thief

But thieves must not be winners
They must not claim the glory
We WILL defeat this virus
And write a brand new story

****

When I first discovered Naked Attraction, I was kind of shocked, but, at the same time, cringingly fascinated. Many months later, my neighbour Ann, accidentally discovered it…. I can remember her text to this day…. "OMG …. I think I've found a porn site on TV...the screen's full of willies!" I had to write a poem……… dedicated to Ann….

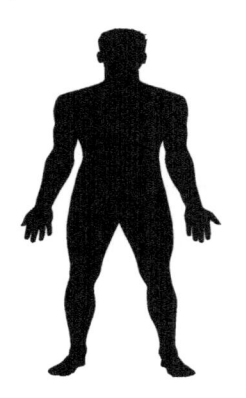

Naked Attraction

I thought I'd watch some telly
Before I go to bed
Fed up with News at Ten now
So what is on instead?

I do some channel hopping
But…wait! What's this I see?
Have I accessed a porn site?
It looks like it to me!

The screen is full of todgers!
All colours, shapes and sizes!
Is this a willy contest?
Are they out to win prizes?

I'd better check the TV Times
To see just what I'm viewing
I really can't believe it!
Whatever are they doing?

It's Channel 4 I'm watching
It's called Naked Attraction
Like good old Cilla's Blind Date
But with a bit more action

The woman's got to choose a man
Based on his naked body!
Well, maybe I'm old fashioned, but
Is that not a bit shoddy?

Oh, now she's getting closer
She really is quite keen
I know just what my Gran would say…
"This really is obscene!"

The woman's put her specs on
She's in there for the kill!
I don't know why I'm watching this
It's making me feel ill…

"Oh that one is too hairy…
And that one's a bit bent…
And that one's just plain scary…
Now that one's heaven sent!"

I really can't take any more
It's making me feel sick
But which one will she go for?
Harry?.... Tom?.... or Dick?

Oh, now we've got the girls on
I think it's getting worse,
I haven't seen this many 'bits'
Since I worked as a nurse!

The bloke's turn now to study…
With no doubt, good intention
If it's not pierced, or waxed, or shaved
It's just not worth a mention!

Now, one has bats tattooed there
She says it's her 'bat cave'
Well, how can you reply to that?
It's certainly his fave!

I think I'd better turn it off
I'm starting to feel faint
What happened to old fashioned charm…
And romance sweet and quaint?

****

This is a true story, of two of the most unpleasant hours of my entire life!

Pamper Session

I thought I'd bagged a bargain
A two hour 'pamper' session
A real cheap deal on Groupon
Boy! Did I learn my lesson!

I set off nice and early....
I've not been there before
I find the address given....
Can this be the right door?

This looks like it's a wig shop
Perhaps I've got it wrong
I'll go inside and ask them
It shouldn't take me long

"It's on the floor above 'Duck'....
You need to go upstairs....
No workers have arrived yet....
Go up and wait in there"

I sit and look around me
I peer into the gloom
I'm sure this is a hair salon
But where's the beauty room?

No sign of doors connecting
Can't even see a screen
What is this place I've come to?
I'm not sure it's too clean

I hear someone approaching
The therapist arrives
She comes in like a whirlwind....
I take her by surprise

She doesn't look professional
I start to feel uncertain
But then she says she's ready
And pulls back a thin curtain

I follow her into a space....
You could not swing a kitten
I think I've made a big mistake
I've had my fingers bitten

I take most of my clothes off
And climb up on the couch
I try to 'think of England'
But wait a minute "Ouch!"

She's certainly not gentle....
In fact she rubs too hard
What's that she's smearing on my leg?
...Feels like a lump of lard!

Where is the soothing music?
Where are the scented oils?
I think I'd feel less anxious
If someone lanced my boils!

The hair salon's in action
The radio, hairdryers,
Two of the stylists falling out....
Calling each other liars

A bell rings near the curtain....
She leaves me lying here....
I wonder where she's going
Then, this is what I hear....

"I need my eyebrows threading"
She says she'll do the job
I'm lying here in just my pants....
She earns a few more bob!

I really can't believe it
The whole thing is absurd....
Then she picks up where she left off
Without a single word

She asks me to turn over
I do....with dread and fear
"And would you like your boobs done?"
Please get me out of here!!

It's now time for the facial
I think she's used goose grease
Perhaps I'm in a nightmare
From which there's no release

Another interruption....
A lady offers cash....
It won't take very long though....
A quick wax of moustache

I really want to leave now....
I just can take no more
At last, the 'pamper's over....
I'm heading for the door

I feel like I've been tortured
I feel completely stressed
I'm oily and feel dirty
My hair a greasy mess

I drive home like a demon
Can't wait to leave this town
I need a shower to cleanse me
A brandy to calm down

Just watch those bargain vouchers....
Might not be what they seem
Next time I'll go for luxury
And hopefully a dream!

****

Does anyone else feel that when you want to buy something these days... there's sometimes just too much choice.... and so it takes ages to decide what you want? Sometimes.... less is more I think….

Tinned Tomatoes

A supermarket 'quick trip'
I'll just nip swiftly in
Now....what was it I wanted?
Oh yes!...... Tomatoes..... .tinned!

I track down their location
I look upon the shelf
There must be fifteen brands here!
Which one? ..... I ask myself

So......do I choose the plum ones?
Or chopped ones, fine, or chunky?
Or what about organic?
Now they sound kind of funky….

But then, there's one with basil
And even some with chilli!
With onions, garlic, olive oil
Now this is getting silly!

I just need tinned tomatoes
It shouldn't be this tricky
I don't know what I want now
I'm starting to get picky

Why are some so pricey?
Why are some so cheap?
The cost of the top range ones
Could make a grown man weep!

I feel all hot and bothered
I've been here half an hour
I just can't make my mind up
I need an ice cold shower!

I finally just grab a tin
I'll just hope for the best
Now.... let me find the gin aisle....
I'm starting to feel stressed!

****

As 'lockdown' measures were relaxed, and shops and pubs started to open, there was a sense of anxiety and uncertainty amongst many people, who did not necessarily yet feel ready to leave their homes.

It's Okay

The world is opening up now
The brave will pave the way
They'll test the new procedures
To check that it's okay

But if you feel uncertain
And up and down each day
Not ready yet to face the world
Please know….. That it's okay

It's okay to feel anxious
Uneasy, tense and scared
The world is looking different
And you need to be prepared

The businesses…they beckon us
To shop, eat, drink, and play
If you think it's too soon for that
Please know….. That it's okay

There is no black and white in this
Just several shades of grey
Please take your time and soldier on
You WILL find your own way

There are no easy answers
On how to cope each day
And if you're too afraid just yet
Please know….. That it's okay

Surround yourself with good things
Dig out your favourite clothes
Put on some happy music
And exercise your toes

Prepare your favourite dinner
Enjoy a bubble bath
Do what you can to ease your day
To get back on the path

One fine and sunny morning
You'll feel like making hay
You'll get yourself back out there
And you WILL be okay!

****

During the Covid19 'lockdown', many people turned to online shopping…..

Online Shopping

Oh I do like online shopping....
You can do it anywhere
You can purchase almost anything
Without a thought or care

Oh I do like online shopping....
You can do it in the nude
If you did that on the High Street
They would think you were quite rude

Oh I do like online shopping....
You can do it in the park
And if you stay out long enough
You can do it in the dark

Oh I do like online shopping....
You can do it in the car
But don't do it whilst you're driving
As you might not get too far

Oh I do like online shopping....
You can do it up a tree
You can get a bird's eye view of things
Whilst on a spending spree

Oh I do like online shopping....
You can do it in your bed
So forget the Kama Sutra....
You can buy some shoes instead

Oh I do like online shopping
You can do it on the loo
You can order prunes and laxatives
Whilst trying to have a poo

Oh I DON'T like online shopping
My bank statement's just arrived
Please disconnect my internet
I need to get a life!

****

I was lazing in the garden .... I overheard a snippet of conversation from someone walking by .... "well.....when you've talked about the teachers and the weirdos who haven't turned up.... what have you got left in common?"..... I assumed they were talking about a School Reunion..... so there was my inspiration!

School Reunion

The good old 'School Reunion'....
A funny sort of 'do'
A place to chat and reminisce
With people you once knew

A chance for some to show off....
To boast how well they've done....
To make some feel inferior
And wish they'd never come

That schoolgirl crush remembered
With fond romantic feelings
Well....now he's fat and balding
And not quite so appealing

That tarty girl who let the boys
Kiss her behind the bike shed
She's just an older trollop now
She can't stay in her own bed

That snotty kid with runny nose
Who never had a hanky
Well he's turned up.... a bit unkempt....
In fact he looks quite manky

And what about that 'know it all'
Who everybody hated
He's here with his big ego now....
It needs to be deflated

You've not seen them for forty years
You'd just about forgot 'em
So once you've recapped on old times
What do you have in common?

There's probably a reason
That you didn't stay in touch
In fact if you're quite honest....
You never liked them much

Of course there will be friendships
That have flourished, grown, and thrive
You don't need a reunion....
'Cause they're still in your life!

Perhaps it's best to leave the past
Just where it's meant to be
And keep your childhood classmates
A distant memory

****

This is a poem about the most expensive holiday we ever had.... and probably the least enjoyable! It was to celebrate my partner's 60th birthday..

Harley Holiday

We book a 'Harley Holiday'
A 'Special Birthday' treat
A pricey celebration
Advancing years to greet

We fly off to the 'Sunshine State'
But hang on ....where's the sun?
It's cloudier than Manchester!
I think that we've been 'done'

The unexpected cold spell
Is causing quite a rumpus
The headline on the evening news....
Miami's wearing jumpers!

We set off to the bike hire place
A Harley trike is waiting
We must dress up in all the gear....
It looks like armour plating

I force myself into the suit
With lots of grunts and cusses
Don't look like sexy biker chick....
More.... Olive.... 'On the Buses'

We waddle out to find the trike
But wait! There's some mistake!
A Honda Goldwing's sitting there
No Harley!......It's a fake!

We booked a 'Harley Holiday'
So we don't want this farce....
I phone the rental car depot
"Do you have any cars?"

They tell us to be there at one
The bike folks now feel bad
They take us to the rental place
But.....'Oh no! .....This is mad!'

We're at the wrong location!
It's not the one I phoned!
We taxi to the right depot
(I feel like going home)!

They say they have no car for us
My heart sinks to my knees
I get upset...they find us one
We head off for 'The Keys'

....And so does everybody else!
It takes us several hours
We find our luxury hotel
And have hot steamy showers

It's absolutely freezing
So we have to eat inside
I wish I'd brought my winter coat
I really could just cry!

Tomorrow it's his birthday
We're going to Key West
Romantic sunset cruise is booked
I'd picked the very best!

The day dawns cold, and windy
Key West is looking grey
The sea is very choppy
No birthday cruise today!

My throat starts to feel achy
The next day I feel ill
We head off to another Key
The weather cooler still

Now both of us are feeling bad
We cannot even eat!
We're staying here in luxury
But can't enjoy the treat

We take our bags down to the car....
Come back to check the room
The key won't work....can't get back in
They've checked us out too soon?

I head off to reception....
Get a replacement key
I get back after walking miles
But still...... there's no entry

They have to find a janitor
.... Have to remove the door
I've really had enough of this
I can't take any more!

At last we're sitting on the plane
But wait!....A problem!....Why?
That's it! .... The plane is going to crash!
And we are going to die!

This birthday we'll remember
But not in the right way
When it's my 'Special Birthday'
I'm NOT going away

****

Sometimes, during conversation, we can just get 'hold of the wrong end of the stick'

A Verse

There are long ones, there are short ones,
Some are narrow, wide, or knobbly
There are those that are quite rigid
Some are flexible and wobbly

Some are smooth and some are spotty
There are those unkempt and hairy
There are crooked ones and straight ones
Some are cute and some are scary

Some are stuck where they're not wanted
Some are photographed in poses
Well I don't know what you're thinking of
But I'm describing noses!

****

Generally, I have the greatest respect for cyclists; however, there seems to be those amongst them who have no manners when it comes to approaching walkers on the same path. I have experienced several 'scary moments' whilst out walking with friends, due to cyclists giving no warning of their speedy approach. I do not understand why they do not legally have to have bells on their bikes. Thank you to those who do have bells and use them....that's all it takes.....a little 'ding a ling'!

Dear Cyclist

Dear cyclist on the footpath
Please let us know you're there
You fly past us in such a rush
And give us quite a scare

Dear cyclist on the footpath
When you zoom from the back
We do a dance and pee our pants
Or have a heart attack!

Dear cyclist on the footpath
When you speed from the rear
You spook the dogs and those who jog
And could cause diarrhoea!

Dear cyclist on the footpath
Please give your bell a ring
We don't have eyes in our backsides....
Can't hear you pedalling

Dear cyclist on the footpath
If you don't have a bell
Then you can't 'ding'...so ....next best thing
Just give a friendly yell....

A quick "excuse me ladies"...
Or.... "Cyclist coming through"!
Then we could slide off to the side
And make some space for you

Dear cyclist on the footpath
Please go and buy a bell.....
Then you can ring your 'ding a ling'
And then all will be well!
****

During 'lockdown' we were being encouraged to improve our fitness and start cycling......inspiration for another poem.....all true I'm afraid ...

On Yer Bike!

Dear Boris! I can't do it!
Unless you want me dead!
Just thinking of a bicycle
Fills me with fear and dread

I have no sense of balance
Not since I was a child
I even get a bit upset
When climbing over stiles

The icy paths in winter
….. I know I'm gonna fall
I once fell into stinging nettles
…..sitting on a wall!

I've tried to ride a bike you see
On one of those nice trails
It's like a magnet draws me
To people, dogs, and snails

I just end up in panic
My feet go to the ground
My calves are turning black and blue
….. the pedals going round

….. Once hired an adult tricycle
Now that was quite good fun!
Until one of the wheels flew off
…. I landed on my bum!

I'm pleased to say I'm not obese
So Boris…. 'on yer bike!'
I'll do my bit and will keep fit
But I'll just 'take a hike!'
****

I really love to go out walking, either on my own or with friends. During the pandemic, I did quite a bit of 'socially distanced' walking with my neighbour, and friend, Ann.....

Walking

I like to go out walking
It makes me feel calmer
But when I go with my friend Ann
There always is a drama!

We once strolled down the Coach Road
Along to Butterley
We heard a crack and both looked back
To see a fallen tree!

Just a few seconds sooner
And we would have been squashed!
Relaxing stroll along the lane?
Our lives could have been lost!

We went a walk down Newlands Road
We picked a lot of litter
All of this 'lockdown exercise'
....In old age we'll be fitter!

That's if we get to live that long
I do begin to wonder....
I'm trying to grab a lager can....
I hear a sound like thunder

Two cars have crashed right next to us!
Just yards from where we're standing!
One's in the air on just two wheels!
....Then falls to a safe landing

We check to see that no one's hurt
....Just lots of angry shouting
We went for a relaxing walk....
Not this traumatic outing!

Our latest trip round Felley way....
We got joined by a bloke
He looked perfectly normal
But oh no! What a joke!

He said there is no Covid....
It's all just one big con!....
And on 15th of August....
We'll have a new king....John

"The Royals are all dead now
Together with George Clooney"
Another so called calming walk
....We've met a raving loony!

He says there'll be no taxes....
Under good old King John
......And life will be fantastic
Well... I say... bring it on!

I don't want to annoy him
So I just let him chat....
I sense that Ann is getting cross....
She thinks he is a prat!

She asks him if he's taking drugs
And what books he's been reading?
I just wish he would disappear
To where is all this leading?

He says we will believe him
When all this comes to light
And so he goes off on his way
And we complete our hike

He leaves us feeling quite disturbed...
Another walking drama!
So we head home for G & Ts
To make us feel much calmer

I think I might 'be busy'
For Ann's next walking caper
.... might even take up cycling now
It just might turn out safer!

****

There is obviously much negativity about 'Social Distancing' so I am trying light heartedly to find some positives..

Positive

There must be something positive
With 'Social Distance' Measures
Some of life's more unpleasant things
Can have their hidden pleasures

Your hairy chin can sprout a bit
Your eyebrows go unplucked
Your make up can be minimal
Aim for the 'natural' look

Your legs can go unshaven
No one can see they're hairy
Your moustache can run rampant
And no one think it scary

Your breath can be more whiffy
Eat garlic all day long
Your armpits can be sweaty too
No one will smell the pong

Don't need to be so cosy
With folks you'd rather not
Your blackheads won't be noticed
No need to squeeze that spot

Don't have to hug the 'huggy' folks
Who you would rather shun
You could go hug a tree instead
They say it's rather fun

No need to offer lifts to folks
You'd rather leave behind
Just mention 'social distancing'
Then you won't seem unkind

You can be anti-social now
Without appearing rude
Don't have to mix with anyone
If you're not in the mood

First dates are more romantic now
Build up to that first kiss
A chance to get to know him well
But not go back to 'his'

You see it's not all doom and gloom
You've got to make the best
Of what can only be described
As one almighty mess!

****

I don't know a huge lot about angling and fishing, but I can imagine that it is a very relaxing pastime, and maybe a good way of getting away from the hubbub of domestic life and troubles ....I couldn't sleep one night, but this was running around my head..... especially after I heard a cockerel calling several times.....

Gone Fishing

To sleep he was unable
His mind a bit unstable
A note left on the table....
'Gone fishing .... Down the res'

He's having quite a battle
To sort out all his tackle
But feels free of the shackle....
'Gone fishing .... Down the res'

A brand new day is dawning
The night turns into morning
A coot cries out a warning....
'Gone fishing .... Down the res'

He hears a pigeon cooing
A cockerel cock-a-dooing
He has a cuppa brewing....
'Gone fishing .... Down the res'

The healthy are out running
The sunrise is just stunning
This plan was very cunning....
'Gone fishing .... Down the res'

A cyclist smoothly riding
The swans come by a gliding
No rules to be abiding....
'Gone fishing .... Down the res'

He feels himself relaxing
The morning gently passing
Away from question asking....
'Gone fishing .... Down the res'

The heron is out stalking
The ramblers are out walking
He wishes they'd stop talking....
'Gone fishing .... Down the res'

The day is getting warmer
He is now feeling calmer
Away from household drama....
'Gone fishing .... Down the res'

A time to sit and ponder
And maybe then feel fonder
Of those he's left back yonder....
'Gone fishing .... Down the res'

A day of quiet angling
His thoughts have been untangling
No longer feels like strangling....
'Gone fishing .... Down the res'

He heads back home to sorrow
The same routine to follow
But can come back tomorrow....
'Gone fishing .... Down the res'

****

As it says in the old song 'What's the use of worrying?.... It never was worthwhile'……..

Don't Worry!

"You die if you worry!
You die if you don't!
So....no point in worrying"
My Grandma would quote

She does have a point there
I know that it's true
So try to be mindful
When life gets to you

No problem is bettered
If you fret and stress
So calmly think how you
Can deal with the mess

It will not get sorted
If you scream and shout
You need to consider
How to work it out

If you feel you're struggling
Then ask for some help
You don't have to sort it
All out by yourself

Some things are much harder
To try to control
And sometimes it's better
To just let things roll

As humans we're programmed
To get through this life
We are built to tackle
The trouble and strife

So stop all that worrying
Not good for your health!
So very important
Be kind to yourself!

Remember my Grandma
When life 'gets your goat'
"You die if you worry....
"You die if you don't!"

****

I really have no idea why this bit of nonsense came into my head.....I think I was becoming a bit 'Lockdown Loopy'

KEEP CALM
AND
CARRY ON

Important Jobs

When World War 2 unfolded
Some were not called to serve
If they had an 'Important Job'
Their home life was preserved

This led to some discussion
Amongst the household ranks….
The things folks took for granted
For which they gave no thanks

"I'm needed" said the chamber pot
And hid beneath the bed
"To serve when calls of nature strike
And wake a sleepy head"

"I'm needed" said the candlestick
"To brighten up the night
To lead the way beneath the stairs
Where people hide in fright"

I'm needed" said the cooking pot
"To put the rabbit stew in
To eke out all the rationing
For which they've done the queuing"

"I'm needed" said the radio
"To bring the household news
And cheer them up with lively tunes
To chase away the blues"

"I'm needed" said the fireplace
"To keep the home fires burning
To warm the children whilst they play
And keep the cats a-purring"

"I'm needed" said the dolly tub
"The washing still needs doing....
They'll need me for the 'poncher' and
.....To put the Dolly Blue in"

So when we say 'Important Jobs'
Just think of how you're living
Life could be much more difficult
So let's have some thanks giving!

****

I'm sure I'm not the only person who sometimes gets a shock when they look in the mirror…..

Mirror Mirror

Mirror Mirror on the wall….
It seems you've been mistaken
The image that you give to me
Is of someone forsaken

Mirror Mirror on the wall….
You're harsh and quite unkind
Why do you paint a picture
Of cheeks and eyes so lined?

Mirror Mirror on the wall….
I think you're mean and nasty!
My peachy fresh complexion
Looks like a Cornish pasty!

Mirror Mirror on the wall….
Just what game are you playing?
My lovely locks of auburn hair
Have gone and now are greying

Mirror Mirror on the wall....
Just tell me...what's your plan?
The woman I am staring at
Reminds me of my Gran!

Mirror Mirror on the wall....
Why are you being ruthless?
The person looking back at me
Looks old, and rough, and toothless

Mirror Mirror on the wall....
You will become unhung
And then the face behind my eyes
Will stay forever young!

****

I live in a house built in 1795, and often wish that I could step back in time, and observe daily life here in times gone by. The fireplace in my dining room must have seen a lot over the years......so I wrote this on behalf of my fireplace......

The Fireplace
(Home Is Where The Hearth Is)

I've been here for two hundred years....
In fact.... a few years more
I've always had the same old view....
A window and three doors

There's usually been a table here....
And oh so many chairs....
Plain wooden ones and cushioned ones....
And ones stuffed with horsehair

At first, I was so occupied....
I cooked, I boiled, I blazed....
My duties are much simpler now....
I just work on cold days

I've witnessed births, I've witnessed deaths....
Watched people fight and struggle
I've also seen them making up....
With kisses and a cuddle

There's been a million cups of tea
With biscuits, toast, and cakes....
Two hundred thousand meals I've seen....
Served up on endless plates

I've helped to fill the old tin bath
And supervised the scrubbing....
I've helped to get the washing dry
After the 'dolly tubbing'

I've watched the families come and go....
I've heard so many stories
I've warmed them through their times of woe....
And cheered at all their glories

So many folks have sat with me....
They've knitted, darned and sewn
They've read their books and dried their hair....
They've gossiped, cried, and moaned

They've smoked their pipes and drank their beer
And put the world to rights....
Played games of cards and dominoes....
And talked into the night

More than two hundred Christmases....
Of people making merry....
The puds I've boiled, the cakes I've baked....
The drinking of the sherry

Children have played upon the rugs....
So many legs I've toasted....
The cats and dogs have gathered here....
Their bellies warm and roasted

I've seen the fashions come and go....
The hemlines rise and fall....
The pinafores, the knee length drawers....
I've surely seen it all!

I've listened to the radio....
To music, songs, and news....
To gramophones and stereos
Alexa and ITunes

Penny Farthings, bicycles....
So many new inventions....
The cars, and trams and railways
The birth of aviation

I've warmed the room for birthday teas
.... All kinds of celebrations....
Romantic dinners, jubilees...
And even coronations

There've been so many Kings and Queens....
Too many wars so epic....
Industrial revolution.....
And now a world pandemic

What's next? I wonder to myself....
As 'lockdown' ebbs and flows
How long will I be standing here?
The truth is.... no one knows

So much has changed in all this time
But some things stay the same....
And everyone I've ever met
Has loved my timeless flames

So I'll remain and proudly serve
All interested parties....
Secure in knowing through all time....
That 'home is where the hearth is'

****

The mention of 'knee length drawers' in my previous poem set me thinking about the history of underwear……it was interesting researching the subject! Although if anyone were to take my computer and look at my browsing history, they might be slightly concerned about my intentions!

'Pants'

The history of underwear...
A subject that is 'pants'!
A thing you seldom think about...
Well now you have the chance!

In prehistoric caveman days...
They hunted in all weathers...
Protected their cold dangly bits...
With loincloths made of leather

In ancient Egypt, linen cloths...
Were used to cover theirs...
They found ...in Tutankhamen's tomb...
Over one hundred spares!

The Middle Ages brought us 'braies'...
A type of longish short...
The Romans had a similar thing...
(More stylish I'd have thought)

A sort of 'onesie'...'union suit'...
Designed by someone savvy...
This had a useful buttoned flap...
For visits to the 'lavvy'

The jockstrap was invented then...
For cyclists as they rattled...
Along the bumpy, cobbled streets...
Protecting 'wedding tackle'

The long johns kept the workers warm...
As did, the old string vest...
The 'boxers' kept them cooler...
But Calvin Kleins' are best!

Now the ladies went 'commando'...
For centuries untold...
No waxing of the 'nethers' then...
So ...didn't feel the cold!

Now let's not 'beat about the bush'...
This was not too hygienic...
Although if they did handstands...
It could have been quite scenic!

They did move on to 'open drawers'...
An early 'crotchless' fashion...
'Suppose it made it easier...
For times of urgent passion!

Attempts to get a 'waspie' waist...
Brought whale bones in a corset...
The lacing up with feet in backs...
They really had to force it!

Chemises, shifts and petticoats...
Bustles, bloomers, lace...
Pantalettes and bodices...
Kept everything in place

The corsets went...the girdles came...
The brassiere enhanced...
In wartime, silk from parachutes ...
Was used to make new pants!

At Wimbledon, in 'forty nine...
A cause for lots of snickers...
Was 'Gorgeous Gussie' showing off...
Her fancy frilly knickers!

Since then there's nothing you can't find...
Bras.... under wired or strapless...
Minimiser, maximiser...
Push up, plunge or backless!

To choose a pair of knickers now...
You need an entire morning!
There's such a vast variety...
It almost becomes boring...

There's mini briefs and maxi briefs...
There's coloured, flowered, lacy...
Bikini, G Strings, shorts and thongs ...
And some are just plain racy!

The bony, rigid, corset's gone...
But now we have the 'Spanx'...
To hold in all our flabby bits...
Well I say ... 'Err...no thanks!'

Some of these things may look the part...
But are they really comfy?
And if your figure's less than great...
Your bum can look quite lumpy!

In later life, when comfort rules...
You don't need cause for moans...
It seems to me you just need 'pants'...
Like good old Bridget Jones!

****

Apart from the odd limerick many years ago, I only started writing poems during the Covid19 'lockdown', in April 2020……..but then just couldn't stop!

Just Words

I think I may have been possessed...
By words that put me to the test...
They even wake me from my rest!
.....Just words!

I know just when it all began...
A comment from my neighbour Ann...
And so my mind ....it ran and ran...
.....Just words!

Oh crikey!....Here I go again!
Fetch me some paper and a pen!
I never know just where or when...
.....Just words!

Is this a blessing, gift or curse?
My thoughts all turning into verse?
I think that I might need a nurse!
.....Just words!

I'm glad that I have got the time
To try to write something sublime
A poem that will flow and rhyme
.....Just words!

If this goes on until I die....
Will I find out the reason why?
Before I have to say goodbye...
....Just words!

****

I absolutely love where I live…..I came here when I took early retirement and it is a truly special place, when I walk out of my back gate, it nourishes my soul.

Special Neighbour

At the bottom of my garden
Cromford Canal resides
A place so steeped in history
True wonders it provides

I think about its working life
The barges towed by horses
Transporting limestone, coal and iron
Throughout the water courses

It's been retired for many years
Now, Nature's taken over
With trees and plant life everywhere
Reeds, bulrushes, and clover

The water teems with wildlife
With crayfish and tadpoles
With newts and toads, and dragonflies
Birds, pike, and water voles

The kingfisher flies swiftly by
The stalking heron waits
The busy moorhens, grebes and coots
The swans with lifelong mates

The air is full of fragrant scents
From blossoms, herbs, and flowers
I lose myself amongst it all
And minutes turn to hours

The seasons change, and life goes on
The wildlife still surviving
Each day brings new and wondrous signs
That everything is thriving

Where once the working horses trod
The nature lovers roam
Dog walkers, joggers, bicycles
Tired ramblers heading home

I wander through this paradise
It calms my busy mind
A better medicine prescribed
I'm sure you'll never find

At the bottom of my garden
Cromford Canal resides
An extremely special neighbour
To have right by my side

******

As September 2020 arrived, and we said goodbye to a very strange Covid19 Summer, the weather was still lovely and I wrote this……..

The Cycle

Farewell faded Summertime
You're leaving us too soon
You'll be reborn in nine months time
Upon the first of June

The red carpet will be laid out
To welcome you once more
With open arms we'll take you in
Your presence we adore

Meanwhile we'll greet your sisters
Meet Autumn, Winter, Spring
We'll celebrate the wondrous things
That every season brings

For now, we welcome Autumn
With all her colours bright
The jewelled trees with falling leaves
And cloudless starry nights

She'll send us teatime sunsets
And longer cooler nights
We'll start to light the log burners
And sit in candlelight

Pumpkins, apples, Halloween
Ghostly treats and tricks
Devils, zombies, skeletons
Witches on broom sticks

Bonfire parties, fireworks
Light up the darkened sky
Hot dogs, toffee, mushy peas
Penny for the Guy?

Oktoberfest and Thanksgiving
'The Trailing Of The Sheep'
Moon and Harvest Festivals
All memories to keep

She'll pave the way for Wintertime
We have nothing to fear
So let's enjoy and say thanks for
The cycle of the year.

****

I was vacuuming one day……and off I went again!

Housework

What is the point of housework?
A never ending job!
I think that I might give it up....
Become a lazy slob!

You flick your feather duster....
Removing old cobwebs
You know that spider's watching you....
He's really not impressed!

You vacuum all the carpets....
You polish wooden floors....
And then the cats and dogs come in
With filthy dirty paws!

You plump up all the cushions....
And tidy up the throws
Someone sits down.... moves them around....
You almost come to blows!

You smooth the sheets and duvets....
Leave pillows all aligned
But all this work will be undone....
When it becomes bedtime

You put away the clothing....
In closets and in drawers
You know that by tomorrow....
You'll find it on the floors!

You clean your kitchen windows....
You make them shine and gleam
But then you start the cooking....
And cover them with steam!

You clean inside your oven....
Into its depths you plunge
Just how does it accumulate?....
All of this grease and gunge!

You wash the pots from lunchtime....
You put them all away
And then it's time for dinner....
It's just like Groundhog Day!

You wipe the kitchen worktops....
You clear up all the grime
You know you'll do it all again....
In just a few hours time!

You sort the dirty laundry....
It really is quite yucky
You wash and steam.... it's all pristine....
And then it just gets mucky!

You scrub the bathroom basin....
This time is such a waste
Before too long someone will come....
And smear it with toothpaste!

You disinfect the toilet bowl....
You leave it looking pretty
Then some kind loved one comes along...
And leaves it rather........!

It really is quite pointless...
All of this toil and strife
I think I know just what I need ...
An old fashioned 'housewife'!

****

I felt angered and worried by the attitude of some people amongst us, who seemed to think that it was ok for them to do just exactly as they pleased, and took little or no notice of the Covid19 rules and guidelines in place. Do they not realise that if we had all adopted that mindset, then we'd just be back at square one? It seems to me that common sense, self discipline and patience is sadly lacking for some.

Why?

Why are they selfish in their ways?
Why don't they seem to care?
Why is life cheapened so today?
Why are they not aware?

Why do they think it's all a game?
Why do they break the rules?
Why aren't they feeling full of shame?
Why do they act like fools?

Why do they think that they're immune?
Why do they feel exempt?
Why are they in their own cocoon?
Why do they Covid tempt?

Why is it they don't understand?
It hasn't gone away!
It's lurking all around the land...
To pounce upon its prey!

This virus loves these carefree types
Within this modern culture...
It's waiting for the chance to strike
Just like a hungry vulture!

Will it become more clear to them?...
When someone they adore
Is lying curtained in the crem
Or scarred for evermore?

****

My favourite comment on this was "Where there's a will there's a relative"

Entitlement

Now, Aunty had a brother
They never did get on
She really didn't like him much
But now he's dead and gone

He left behind a daughter
Who took after her Dad
So Aunty didn't see her much
'Cause she was just as bad

Now, Aunty had some good friends
She never was a wife
She didn't have a family
But led a happy life

She loved all furry creatures
Especially her cats
They helped to keep her company
And kept away the rats

She was a lovely lady
She did have some romance
She'd go abroad and travel lots
Go walking, skate and dance

Now, Aunty's life is over
She's gone to rest in peace
Friends weeping by the graveside
.....And then appears the niece....

She's spent all Daddy's money
And now comes uninvited
To claim her huge inheritance
To which she feels 'entitled'

'Cause Aunty..... She was loaded
She never had a daughter
So clearly, she would get it all!
The cash, and bricks and mortar

She'd buy a brand new sports car
She'd go to St Tropez
She'd really live the high life
She'd eat and drink and play

She waits with baited breath now
Just how much will it be?
(She must be worth a fortune)
And all for 'Me! Me! Me!'

So ....Aunty's Will is opened....
Well isn't it a shame?
For nowhere on this document...
Is written niece's name!

So much for her 'entitlement'
Well isn't it a pity?....
She's left it to the cat's home
To help the homeless kitties!

****

Just to say... Of course, I know you can have true friends on Facebook too!

Facebook Friends

I don't have any Facebook friends
I like mine to be 'real'
But since this Covid's dragging on
It might change how I feel

It seems with all the rules out there
That change from day to day
Then having friends on Facebook now
Might be the safest way

I suppose they have their good points
These 'social media mates'
At least you can delete them when
They start to irritate

You don't have to invite them round
When you would rather not
If they start to upset you....then....
'Block' them.... and off they trot!

You could have a 'Zoom' meeting with
The ones you like the best
Where you can chat and gossip too
And 'get it off your chest'

I don't think that it's quite the same
If you can't have a hug
But 'Social Distancing' is here
To keep away 'the bug'

I think that on reflection now
I'll stick with 'rule of six'
And see my friends in person still
To get my friendship fix

We have to keep ourselves apart
But we can see our smiles
True friendship will keep us all sane
And beats Facebook by miles!

****

Boris Johnson stated that 'a stitch in time saves nine!'

A Stitch In Time

"A stitch in time saves nine" says Boris....
So grab your thread and needle
We now all need to stitch together
To save us from this evil!

We must cut down on social contact....
Let's try to stem this virus
We need to stop and think of others
Let's make some sacrifices!

We've all just got to be more careful....
We won't die from less boozing
It's not that hard to put a mask on....
The rules don't need abusing!

We've got to try to trust the experts....
They don't want this mess either!
Some think they don't know what they're doing....
But who is any wiser?

Sometimes in life it feels a struggle....
A bit like stormy weather
What's needed now is good old 'teamwork'
To get through this together

For some, Covid might mean no symptoms
For others, just some coughing....
But if you pass it on to granny....
You could just nail her coffin!

So come on England...let's knuckle down!
We really all can do this!
A bit less 'me' and a lot more 'us'
Protecting ALL our futures!
****

At times it seemed that we may never get back to 'normal'. I hope that as you are reading this that the situation has improved.

ONE DAY AT A TIME

What Tomorrow Brings

We're living in uncertain times
With Covid in the wings
We need to have some patience now....
See what tomorrow brings

Our daily lives are upside down
With 'social distancing'
We wear our masks and wash our hands....
See what tomorrow brings

We feel like puppets dancing round
But who's pulling the strings?
We've got to keep a level head....
See what tomorrow brings

Our state of mind and mental health
May well be suffering
We've got to try to understand....
See what tomorrow brings

This virus has no preferences
From paupers through to kings
We need to try to live with it....
See what tomorrow brings

****

This is (mostly) a true story..... So funny at the time. Thank you to my beautiful cat Marmite (sadly no longer with us) and my ex-neighbours and good friends Deb and Steve, and Tilly….. for the content….

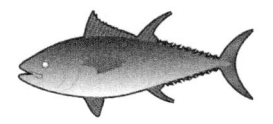

Something Fishy

I bought some cans of tuna fish....
A special type for cats....
My cat sniffed at her dish and thought...
'Well ...I'm not eating that!"

I gave them to my neighbour, Deb....
To try with her cat, Tilly
So off into the fridge they went....
Stuffed next to the Caerphilly

One night her partner Steve came home....
With hunger on his mind....
Perhaps a sandwich would be nice
With salad on the side

He opened up the fridge and found
The items for his snack....
Including tins of tuna fish....
With cheeses at the back

Then Deb came in to find the room
With odour somewhat 'whiffy'
"Your sandwich looks disgusting!"....
Steve thought it a bit "iffy"

But not a man to waste his food....
He ate it anyway....
He then went off to get some sleep
After his busy day

The next morning at breakfast time
Deb found an empty can....
The 'kitty tuna' was no more....
It was inside her man!

Now, Deb is 'fussy' with her food
(She won't eat yellow rice)
So thinking what had happened here....
Well this was just not nice!

"You've eaten Tilly's food you fool!"
She could be heard to call....
Steve had a bowl of 'mew'sli now....
And thought about fur balls

What a 'cat'astrophe! He thought....
As he prepared his lunch
"I think I'll have some nice fish pie....
Or 'Go Cat' for some crunch"

All's well that ends well, so they say
At least most of the time....
Now Deb has got her "purrfect" man....
And Steve is 'feline fine!'

****

I was walking through the trees one day and it started 'raining' acorns....

Instinct

It started raining acorns....
I looked above to see....
A squirrel leaping through the trees....
He looked back down at me

He was collecting free food
To see him through 'til Spring
How can a little creature know
Just when to do these things?

They act upon their instinct....
It's something we have lost....
I can't see us surviving long
Outside in rain and frost

We think we are so clever
With all our fancy 'stuff'
But up against the wildlife
We do not look so tough

We need to learn some lessons....
From Nature all around....
And come back down to Earth a bit
Before we run aground

We think we're so important
But ... see the mess we're in!....
We must respect the wildlife
For they're the ones who'll win!

****

*I was out on a walk with some friends, and saw a sign on a gate.
You never know when inspiration will strike!*

Apple Pie

"Don't take life too seriously....
No one gets out alive"
I saw this sign upon a gate
It's true! No one survives!

So what's the point of living?
If all you do is die?
Well if you really want to know
I think it's apple pie!

With lots of cream or custard....
And then there's treacle sponge
And what about a spotted dick?
Go on now.... take the plunge!

You could have sticky toffee
Or crumble made with plums
Or cornflake tart with crème anglaise
To fatten tums and bums

You might prefer a cheesecake
Or strawberries and cream
Or maybe a profiterole
Is more your dessert dream?

Then there's the sherry trifle
Or maybe Bakewell Tart
And don't forget the chocolate mousse
Where does a person start?

So.... seeing as we're living
We should just heed the sign
As you can see life can be 'sweet'
So bitterness ....decline

For if you think about it....
Feel stressed and you'll be fraught
But turn it round.... it spells desserts
Now that's a better thought!
****

I discovered a type of poetry known as 'looping', where the last word on a line, is also the first word on the next....

Heartache

Don't keep your heartache buried deep
Deep inside your heart
Heartbroken may be how you feel
Feel lost and torn apart
Apart from a few lucky folks
Folks have been in your shoes
Shoes are made for walking
Walking clears the blues
Blues and greens of Nature
Nature has it all
All the blue sky and green leaves
Leaves you walking tall
Tall and strong just like the trees
Trees can help you heal
Heal your breaking heart and then
Then improve how you feel
Feel that you can share your thoughts
Thoughts are better aired
Aired and shared amongst your friends
Friends are there to care
Care and help you through this time
Time for you to mend
Mend your aching, breaking heart
Heartache then will end

******

I'd been a walk around the local 'res' on a perfect mid-September evening after a beautiful sunny warm day…..

September Evening

On this September evening
I walk amidst the trees
The weather is just perfect
With just a breath of breeze

The greens are fading fast now
As Autumn does unfold
And waiting quietly in the wings
Are orange, red, and gold

They'll gently make their entrance
Enveloping the green
The trees with their new outfits
Will brighten up the scene

The show will soon be over
So take the time to see
The picture all around you
The world in true beauty

I thank my lucky stars now
That I can be a part
Of this evolving season
That nourishes my heart

****

It was a beautiful sunny, September afternoon, I took a walk around the reservoir, which I do most days. I never tire of this special place.

Thankful

I'm sitting by the reservoir
The sun is shining down
I must have come at 'bath time'....as
There's splashing all around

The mallards in particular
Are causing quite a scene
And in between her fishing trips
The grebe is keeping clean

Is anything much noisier?
Than hungry baby grebes?
Demanding to be fed 'right now!'
Persistent in their greed

The growing cygnets on the bank
All preening in a row
I swear that they are chatting....as
They watch the scene below

I'm sitting really close to them
They've grown so proud and bold
I've known these five all of their lives
They're less than five months old

I feel so very thankful
For this, my neighbourhood
The res, canal and wildlife
They make me feel so good!

****

Printed in Great Britain
by Amazon